By the same author

By Grand Central Station I Sat Down and Wept
A Bonus
In the Meantime
Necessary Secrets
On the Side of the Angels

Elizabeth Smart

The Assumption of the Rogues & Rascals

FOURTH ESTATE • *London*

Fourth Estate
An Imprint of HarperCollins*Publishers*
1 London Bridge Street,
London SE1 9GF
4thEstate.co.uk

This Fourth Estate paperback edition published 2015
Published by Paladin 1991

Previously published by Panther Books 1980

First published in Great Britain by
Jonathan Cape Ltd
in association with Polytantric Press 1978

1

A catalogue record for this book is available from the British Library

ISBN 978-0-00-815574-2

Typeset in Adobe Garamond Pro by Palimpsest Book Production Ltd,
Falkirk, Stirlingshire
Printed and bound in Grafica Veneta S.p.A., Italy

The Assumption of the Rogues & Rascals

ACKNOWLEDGMENTS

Parts of this book first appeared in *The Fortnightly* (edited by Peter Everett and John Rety, London) and in *Botteghe Oscure* (edited by Marguerite Caetani, Rome), to whom acknowledgments and thanks are due.

PART ONE

After the War

THIS IS THE SCENE

Wandering in the wastes of Kensington, the mean mad faces pass like derelict paper bags. The neat ruins of the war lie like a boring scar, whose history is all of the repetitive future, and all that memory can retain.

It is the autumnal equinox that blows out the pleats of my old tweed skirt. The moon races behind the tall and interminable wilderness of Onslow Gardens. All that was held in by courage and the ardour of people's prayer to be good is loose now, and makes a lunatic and evil ghost to lurk in the trodden Squares.

There is no gas; there is no fuel; there is very little food. Also, there is still the demand for our pity for the poorer, the colder, the hungrier.

Cats are the freest beings, for very few people bear them any resentment. The foolish dogs waddle and trot about, unaware of how indelicately they expose the regrets and longings of their owners. The cheap sparrows peck about in the dust.

This is the scene for the drama which we are now too tired to perform. Christ how tired we are. Every article in the great cold room of the landlady's flat has a different floral design. There are only remnants left over from her previous lives. She is making a fresh start in a rehabilitated house, which was only slightly damaged by blast, and now is made into flats. But really she is unable to make a fresh start, and her tired heart spends its holiday from the queues moping about her daughter who is in Leeds, waiting for her second baby to be born and her husband to be demobbed. The appearance of my landlady's hope is only reflex action.

Women with strained faces are slapping their babies for relief.

The time of repentance is come. Soon even the most obtuse will be able to observe the wickedness of war. Repentance – but also reparation. We will

REPAY. It is guilt that blows icily around corners with the autumnal equinox. The predatory suspicion is dogging us that we cannot, can never, escape the consequences of our orgies. When the door slams during the cinema we realize that there is no retreat. We are meek when bus-girls admonish us, because we are aware of how wrong we have been. But our mildness and our inconspicuous behaviour and our passive resignation will not deceive the Furies. They are adamant, oncoming, and, I fear, we fear, we *know*, will be overpowering.

For we are not massed for victory, and our subjective passions have not made a large image of righteous indignation to be our mirage and our guide. O Führer of self-love and self-hate, whose false moustaches fooled us into thinking he was not us: where is your twin enemy with the terrible banner of peace?

But even this invocation sounds too highfalutin for the times – out of place. I am, after all, just a woman in a fish queue, with her bit of wrapping paper, waiting for her turn. I wouldn't budge an inch out of line for faith, for hope, or for glory.

History is in the fishmonger's hands, and I will be grateful for the stale allotment he allows.

Rising rapidly up the steps of the moving bus, I will not be too proud to mind if my landlady, my boss, or my lover, see the great hole in the heel of my stocking. Vanity has become a burden, and I think desire has failed too. On Bruton Street I saw a lady glancing sideways at the lingerie, with only a mild daydream about what would happen to her if it were hers; not, as it used to be, with the greed that begets action.

I meet kindness, sometimes, but very soft and autumnal it glimmers out in gratitude for an invocation of memory: of a child smiling, of a woman joking, for instance.

And hourly, yes, at every timeless hour, redundant and obsolete, the witches increase in Kensington, as one more woman becomes too weary to go on; too weary to dispel the glaze that has settled over her eyes. They crawl into their holes, where the gas no longer functions.

And winter is coming on.

PART TWO

Signed on for the Duration

This is the scene outside, and it seems to synchronize with the scene within, for it is not at all what a five-year-old child would have seen, chasing his ball in a still-green Kensington Gardens; or what an old man would muse on, sitting in his club, having weathered both kinds of war, and forgotten them all.

But these two categories are outside the story, merely the cosy covers of the book.

What is to happen now?

Out of this weary landscape, girding your strengths around you, you are to step through a couple of decades with your children on your back, singing a song to keep them optimistic, and looking to left and right. For the right and not for the left.

Left right, Left right.

Are you a friend to me, sergeant-major conscience, strictly insisting on keeping in step with the true, the true, the true that you once knew, and not the invented possibilities that reeled in front of your reeling mind when the lightning lit up everything?

You expected a bill, and a bill is what you get. This is the bill. Now pay it.

Left right. Right turn. March into this meadow, heaving your heavy rucksack full of the future, and see what the present brings.

I am friendless, covered in mud, cowardly, weak, untrained. But signed up for the duration.

You brought it upon yourself. You have only yourself to blame.

True. True. Perfectly true. Too late to desert. Too late to heave off your crippling kit and head for the hills. The problem now is how to put one foot forward, never mind best, just foot, foot, foot. Forward. On. Just keeping your feet from going numb. Just keeping them functioning.

In what direction?

Just avoiding the bogs, snipers, snares, enemy propaganda. Taking cover in skirmishes. Using techniques of camouflage. Lying low when the tanks roll out of the woods, squashing all before them.

A couple of decades will see you out of this bondage. A couple of decades will bring honourable discharge.

PART THREE

Working

As I sat by my office window, I observed the generations, who are, after all, only the consequences of someone else's desires, moving with fatuous smiles into traps.

I saw sad fathers and mothers moving patiently aside in buses.

And I saw myself spending my days punching holes in telegrams because of the consequences of my own desires.

I saw myself now ignominiously far from the bellowing Jungfreud with which I once leapt into the arms of circumstance.

And why should I file office books instead of putting my child to bed?

This question arose as I sat by my first office window.

Round and round like a frantic squirrel in a cage I chased it looking for a loophole. I found none. The exits were all blocked. Facts must be your friends, I said.

Panting, bewildered, I looked out to see the other prisoners, generations and generations, moving in a long queue through their unvarying days.

This cliff, I thought, this office block, would certainly suit a suicide.

After work, I dance in smoky nightclubs, swooning to jazzy versions of *Liebestraum*. What if next morning I look from my office window and say, 'Shall I leap over the edge?'

The long fall is appalling.

* * *

Besides, I am afraid of death now, since he sits beside me at dinner parties.

'How do you do, dear one,' I say, wanting above all to be brave, dandified, unobtrusive; to smile like the Spartan boy with the fox gnawing his intestines: saying, 'It's nothing! It's nothing! I don't feel a thing! Pay no attention! Please continue our conversation!'

But I vomit at the side when I notice his decomposing face. Especially in dreams. All feeling shall cease like the grinders and I shall be cold, cold, and everyone will examine my private papers.

Besides, what is the end of the story?

Boring and gory by turns, painful, repetitive, the story goes on, leads where?

Curiosity, ignorance, humility, pride, lead one to take the next step, and the next, and the next.

* * *

Only the prisoner understands the meaning of freedom. What if he speaks with embarrassing passion? What if sometimes his bias is bitter? Little by little such great flapping words come flying home to roost.

Yesterday from my office window I saw a crippled girl negotiating her way across the street, her shoulders squarely braced. At each jerky movement her hair flew back like an annunciatory angel, and I saw she was the only dancer on the street.

All right. We begin. We take our hypothesis: Everyone must work; nobody must loaf. 'Pull your own weight,' my mother repeats. And Henry Vaughan, that dear beauteous jewel, says: 'Keep clean, bear fruit, and wait.'

This seems to cover housework, childbirth, sainthood.

But money must come into it.

One man I saw, though, if I may bring in a feudal loophole before we examine the working proposition, who strung exquisite beads together.

He lived in a tenement and was called Goofy Al. A certain Lady Elixir walked by there one day to take some Robert Greig seedcake to a dying charlady, but didn't know of his existence. Otherwise she would certainly have arranged, by a little more whoring and a little less charring, to have eased the lot of a master craftsman.

And since, then, Lady Elixir's seedcake might have kept poor Al alive, when a public vote would not have; and charity from a less picturesque hand might have warped his mighty spirit, I am reluctant, until we know more, to see the future so drearily laid out like an allotment garden, with each to his patch of work.

It was to work that the serpent hissed them out of Eden.

Adam delved and Eve span.

In their sorrow they brought forth children.

But in Adam's absence, Eve has much to do.

Too much? We'll see.

* * *

It was up those tenement steps where the children sat, waiting for things to happen, and the stale curtains blew out so intimately above the tired geraniums, that I heard a young girl ask: 'Mother, what is happening to my breasts? Two little knobs have appeared.'

Far away, long ago, the first rumbling intimations of the cruel sexual bargain to come.

Once, at my window, looking for relevancies, I saw a church through ferny leaves of a tree, and a five-pointed star embellishing a rooftop venthole.

Faintly I heard the congregation singing. The white sang flat. The black sounded like an orgy. I thought this last might lead somewhere.

Might lead the daughters to the sacred grove?

Maybe.

God likes a good frolic.

But enough. All this is leading us, with unsuitable sighs, to the bird's-eye view, the aftermaths of love and adolescence – that pair we deride when we are impotent and consequently jealous. That's for later.

There are long years to slog through first.

'The spectacle of a young woman so obsessed with her own emotions revolts me.'

Is it possible in the midst of the battle to view the war with a larger perspective?

We'll see.

After being knocked out on the battlefield (of love? of passion? – never mind now), I lay a long time like Lazarus waiting for Jesus to come and tell me to get up. He may have come. Or he may not. Or he may have come and I have moved to another address. Or maybe he kissed me in a spot where too much local anaesthetic lingered. Anyway, there has been no resurrection.

It is not as if I hung upon a cross saying, 'Lord, Lord, why hast thou forsaken me?'; for none of my wounds, if any exist, are bleeding. I sit at a desk in an office, making out shopping lists, adding up my bills.

When Jericho fell, weeping was permitted, and in Babylon it was fashionable to make a memorable moan by the retreating waters. But here you must go to your office, looking sprightly, with a sparkle even if synthetic in your eye. For who dares to stand up and say 'We are weary! O Christ but we are weary!'

I must keep my eye on the object, which is: the annihilation of love, so that love may be suffered; or, rather, the cessation of feeling, so that suffering may be borne, and love, possibly, reborn in a new form.

In the meantime I smell spring flowers, but fail to cry out luscious gratitude like Whitman. If I say, 'My love lies three thousand miles away', that is merely to say, 'It is so many miles from Clapham Junction to London.' If he were here he would be no nearer. If he took me in his arms I should say 'Two bones meet.'

That's a burnt-out comet.

Even though I know, among the other statistics, that the rousable senses lie volcanic underneath, it is not this May that the flowers will sprout on me.

But we are getting away from the object, again, always into this obsessional fog. (I am the obsessional type. Which type are you? If you are the butterfly type you will never forgive my intensity.)

Has anyone ever been this way before? There are no signs.

An obsessional fog, even if it is made of a flock of holy ghosts, is not the sort of thing we can put before the members of Parliament. The domestic details, yes, if suitably arranged, but not the mad moment, not the electric revelations that cause the soul to seize up.

Is it a certain shyness on their part that makes them unable to take in these trembling statistics, too fleshy too flighty too messy for debating floors? Could they be leaving out some crucial bits? They could be. But that's the way they are. Facts must be your friends.

At the corner of the roof, two sparrows make love just outside their nest. The male cleans his beak and looks abroad after each bout. The female, though, quivers and continues to chirp a low note, looking round in fearful expectation for the next act. She is fearful in case there will be no next act, and the future suddenly cease.

PART FOUR

Bearing

I am in England, where I longed to be.

I escaped by a hair's breadth the torpedo that seemed at the time to be a friendly if banal ender of my story. When the alarm sounded, I waited, with my daughter strapped into my lifebelt, full of relief, a kind of wicked joy, that I should be offered such an effortless way out of my pain.

But that was not to be.

Abandoning love as a comfortable kind of completion, a double or nothing; forgetting the nights O the red nights under Brooklyn Bridge; memory must memorize only a way to live or go mad; and forget the rest.

To dare to be born.

To bear love.

Notice how nature makes therapeutically blurred all visions until one has served her purpose. Notice how pregnant women move in a slow stately way as if they were moving in deliberation to the Last Judgment sure of their good marks. They may desire to be avenging and decisive like tigers, but the waters that hang in the womb, cocooning the embryo, cast their influence on their taken-over body too.

Useless to invoke God then. He stands awkwardly aside like a husband at a birth, and nature like a red-cheeked midwife flounces flamboyantly round.

Will you let this rough woman have command, God? Will you leave me to her mercy as she puts dust-sheets over my eyes and folds my mind away? He will. He does.

I try to remember how, when birth comes, the dams will break, and God will assume His majesty and roll in pain like an avenger over my drenched soul, and love and blood flow back into the world.

All this will be, I suppose. But I remember a hole in my body through which the four winds blew cruelly. I remember a vulnerability against which a spring leaf made a too-serious attack. O God I remember your appraising finger going over my ruined but conscious frame.

Waiting for a birth I hear the bells ringing boringly. Church bells, hospital bells, ship's bells. They tell me that boredom is a helpful retreat for the aged. They tell me that the endless repetitions of life and death are soothing, rhyming lullabies, patterns in the jibbering void. They say peace has sometimes been obtained. Pacification is possible. Flesh can be sweet.

But peace and erotics are far far from those parts that now strain like Hercules in labours almost more than they can bear. They are at work! THIS IS WORK! Serious, gigantic, absolute. All other occupations seem flibbertigibbet by comparison with the act of birth. Love and all its flimsy fancies are rolled under this mighty event, rolling all before it: crushed like straw conceits. Even the love of God is steam-rolled aside, as the job that must be done is done.

Thus, in the twentieth century, is born a son of man, while above the agony shrill women request time off to go for a cup of tea. Slapdash he is thrown among the muddle, while harassed apprentices jostle the bloody pans.

But celebrate! Celebrate! Celebrate!

It is not too much to bear a womb.

PART FIVE

The Assumption of the Rogues and Rascals

Out in the garden it is May, but the sun keeps going in, and I have been frustrated too many times to be able to withstand its uncertainty. The lilacs and the fields of buttercups and the birds' eggs in the hedges are mere statistics, like the inventory of a house whose inmates have no meaning or connection, a catalogue of the world, without passion or caprice.

Who can I talk to? Who can I be angry with?

At night, the pressure of my captivity, and my helplessness, make my brain reel, so that I feel dizzy and faint. Rats and rabbits die of indecision when an experiment forces them two ways. Why shouldn't I die from the insolubility of my problems and the untenability of my position?

Nevertheless, on this lovely afternoon, what is left of my youth rushes up like a geyser, as I sit in the sun, combing the lice out of my hair. For it is difficult to stop *expecting* (*What my heart first waking whispered the world was*), even though I am a woman of 31½, with lice in her hair and a faithless lover.

(I remember those long summer evenings you told me about when the holiday music made you nostalgic and restless to go to America and find your bride. Those wastes of Sundays, stretching through the suburban streets, where nothing could ever happen. Mother, may I go now? May I take my ticket and begin? The holidaymakers return from the country with amorous remembrances, because the fields were full of flowers. But the tin music of the organ-grinder reminds them of something late, too late, in beginning.

The days are going by. Nothing has happened. I am too old now to wear a floppy beribboned hat and innocuous sandals. I can no longer carry off the precocious gesture I learnt so well as a child.

Why has no one leaned down out of a waterfall and covered me with blood and bliss?)

I cannot bear the lilac tree now. Even while I look it goes brown. Before I have taken the path across the field it will never be summer again.

After I had given birth to my first child, I felt time and space come whorling back into the empty space where it had lain. And Einsteinian demons came rushing to attack me with the terrible nature of the naked truth. But now I sit in country kitchens, discussing the minor discomforts of childbirth, and the domestic details of love.

Was it for this that so many miracles came roaring like bombers across the wilderness of America?

Down the Pimlico Road and across Ebury Street, the buses cluster like vultures in the open spaces where already forgotten bombs brought disaster. But who listens to history? I too have chilblains and a faithless lover and trouble making ends meet, say the women in the fish and chip queues.

Over the uncooperative landscape, inertias and despairs find their way, make nests in every likely corner, so that none can hold a hopeful surprise which might, at the last trump, have come running with a golden solution held up in a happy finger.

O stop the caterwauling! Women with gusty voices pound pianos in pubs, impossibly happy against great odds. More ravaged and more successful by far than you, they know how to back-slap life with a greeting of gratitude.

I am old enough to know that nothing I want will ever happen. I might get a faded facsimile. If I were lucky a man I want might happen to find comfort in my simple meals, or warmth from a fire always burning at the right moment.

This isn't at all enough, but I see I must make it do. I must. I see I must.

Take a look at the women decorators, sitting cosy on the cushion of time. Their hearts are upholstered in *toile-de-jouy*; they have coromandel screens around their sex; *eau-de-nil* niceties perplex their intellectual faculties, bending and stretching politely in perfect time. What if they lean suspiciously out of their veils? Their gloves are spotless and there are no ladders in their stockings and their shoes are new. Bathmats and clean towels and mushrooms-under-glass await them at regular hours at home. Even though the rain may beat upon their Elizabeth Arden foundations, the wind never wails in desolation near such cheery charm.

Look how they bustle and bristle with energy, exuding capability, lying low to supply a touch of fantasy at fantastic prices to the anxious rich. Poised beside an obelisk, and at the brink of death, a lifetime of restraint and lady-like bulldozery leaves only a mask, crumpled like tissue paper.

A certain resentment remains.

But better than moving up the Pimlico Road in a sloppy fashion: buttons falling off, stocking-ladders widening, nerves jangling.

Do a sleight-of-hand with circumstance.

Supposing you were forty, and decay creaking in every orifice (my dear, why doesn't somebody tell her?): then you might well mock these squandered excruciatingly solitary evenings and say, Oh well, it is to make the pain less intense. It is not.

I've stopped, at its ardent obstreperous source, every hopeful passion, every complete desire, with its attendant, demanding impossibles. There's no *That* and it's all over. Nothing is ever over. I've watched a rogue marry and die, decay and betray, and silently lie and deny. What is under my treacherous scum of a surface?

Pressed below into unbelievable obeisance, lie malformed, undernourished wishes, starved, ill-treated, under a social smile. Not even a tear: for it's years and years beyond that sentimental pillar-of-salt-looking back.

Adamantine truth is an uncomfortable bedfellow: knobbly-kneed, toothy and unkissable.

Can I tolerate myself for these coming twenty years?

Struggle to straighten your stocking seam, woman-of-forty, for a managing director hasn't time for remote causes.

* * *

It's only a simple story: a younger girl usurps the place of the wife. Look in the women's journals and be consoled. The rascal in his taxi burrs up to the door and gives you one wild moment like other people's moments. Then, like a caricature of the sensible being, you will behave with constrained reason and tact, knowing it is only a Brummel's defiance of death, a myth-preservation in the teeth of the hideous facts. For one hour only, rising to the occasion.

Then, lapping, lowering, devouring, like all the wolves in every child's nightmare since the beginning of time, will return the moment of aloneness to be BORNE.

No. No. No. It is not possible. It is not bearable. It isn't a pretty picture. Strut in your scarlet coat. Put perfume behind your ear. Move across the crowded floors of the places where people meet, into restaurants, with an earnest look, to discuss the mathematics of the spirit, moistened with sweet white wine.

* * *

So I took a train to France, saying Ah-hah! I have fooled you, terrible Truth! I can sip a Martini, perfectly at ease with platitude. I can sit in a well-groomed garden, with an elastic girdle holding up my nylons, and never give a thought to the labouring worm below the geraniums.

Perhaps a man with an expensive shirt and Tweed on his moustache will see in me an acquisition for his yacht. I'm toughening. I'll juggle with the boredom of his conversation for the sake of its destination. Or maybe, like a doctor, find excitement in the symptoms beneath the lines and lies.

Cruel with escape, I savour the discomforts of the night train journey, developing an appetite for this new guise of the world. Feeling my apple in the dark, the melting chocolate on my tongue, the stranger's damp socked toe pressing into my sleep, possibilities seethe. Under cover of this crowded breathing, huge horizons emerge, lower and higher and wilder than ever before, like a new division in natural science, found rich and going on under a stone.

What if the man on the yacht is only a fiction?

He is never what is offered by way of a dose, anyway. Six sensible people await me at the villa, in a pocket of security where a rascal has never been seen.

And then unbelievable the holiday sea is thrown like a brilliant gift below the olive trees, where limousine roads are licensed to run shining through. Here fabulous loves without discomfort move into perfumed sleep. And schoolteachers walk along shores in carefully-thought-out wardrobes, deceived into expecting the impossible.

They were all sitting round a table under a cherry tree in the courtyard, adding up and subtracting and dividing the francs that each owed each.

The bougainvillaea and the wistaria and the geraniums were pouring passionate blossom all over the villa, and the sun was dazzling.

Approach these six people in a usual way.

Smile slowly and carefully. Do not ruffle a priceless complacency, inherited from generations of security.

Do not let too much irrelevant and ill-founded happiness wound their incapable spirits. However unequivocally the sun shines, remember they are in their cage of grievance, in seemly mourning for lives laid down a long long time ago.

This thickness is your balm. Behind it you will heal in camouflage.

Sleep is safe. In an alcove of the marble-floored salon, I lie on a camp-bed, drugged by the sinful heat and a precious ration of luxurious sloth. Through the deep layers about me, open to the sprouting of the whole year's shelved desires, I hear them adding and subtracting and dividing, with an edge in their voices, growing shriller, panicking, as the Mediterranean tendencies make a more serious attack.

We stroll down the bare road, pared by years of sun, lapped up lovingly in the blue endless day: an old man with a cardboard face, a friendly couple, two doctors, a disgruntled wife, and me.

'Let's have a coffee.'

'Can we afford it?'

'Let's have a Pernod!'

'Can we afford it?'

'That's two hundred and fifty francs you owe me.'

'That's one hundred and seventy-five francs I owe you.'

'I'll pay you later.'

'We must get back for lunch. I've put the potatoes on.'

'Is there any lettuce left in the larder?'

Smile slowly and carefully. This endless exterior is your remedy. Winkle out the ounce of life. That is the work in hand. It is sweaty excavation. But sometimes viable seeds have been found in Egyptian tombs.

'Is there any lettuce left in the larder?'

'That's two hundred and fifty francs I owe you.'

* * *

Across the bay the tin music reverberates. The dreams of sailors for a moment flash in late night cafés shrilly through the haze. For a moment even the lucky mediocre are caught up lavishly. The music is richly changed by the warm evening and the proximity of nightingales. It is here. It is just across the water and down the still-warm road, rioting, swooning, abundant. (Remember the long summer evenings when the nostalgic music made you restless to go?) Just down the road are mysterious bright-eyed energies, issuing out of alleyways, drinking in smoky corners.

But we sit sedately on the terrace, playing paper games and laughing hysterically at a daring sally.

The evening is young. The evening is insistent. The music is loud and time is going by. Everything is happening. But we are just out of reach.

'Well, I think I'll turn in.'

'I'll pay you the two hundred and fifty francs in the morning.'

'Would you like a cup of cocoa?'

'Is this your banana or mine?'

Can I leave my post, desert this job at hand,

trying, within earshot of the loud summer woods, to warm life into a dinosaur's egg?

'I'm going into the town.'

Is it seemly? Is it right? A conventional reflex stirs, or perhaps the seed beneath the snow, and I walk through the hot dark night with the cardboard Uncle Amos by my side.

In the cave a boy bangs the piano. Other people's loves float through the smoky air, easy and exciting, in a continual state of change.

'I'm worried about my income tax.'

'Shall we have some wine?'

'Well, we might have a half bottle.'

The waiter gave us a whole one.

'It is on me, monsieur.'

'But really, we can't accept it. I never like to be beholden to anyone.'

'Then let me.'

'No. I never give and I never receive. I keep myself to myself.'

'Please let *me. I* don't pay income tax.'

'No, I couldn't. Two hundred and fifty francs is your share. That's half, because the waiter gave us the other. Though I didn't like accepting it. Still, I suppose it pays him. Shocking price though. Have you five francs and that will make it square?'

Back through the dark. The music is over. The bougainvillaeas are breathing in their sleep.

The night is squandered.

It went on like this for days and days and days. As the sun beat down, the doctors grew rosy and brown. They tumbled about on the sand, but it didn't affect their conversation. Uncle Amos murmured that he'd like a little bit of love. But the safeness of his remote world ceased, even by contrast, to console me, since the sun beat up so, overwhelmingly charming. The faces of the rogues and rascals hung mocking and aphrodisiac over Antibes, as I trudged up the road with Uncle Amos, doing acrobatics of adjustment.

When he spoke of his Regency drawing-room and his obedient housekeeper, I remembered the red nights under Brooklyn Bridge. What is the setting, ever, without the act? Death is the price of painlessness.

Do you want a husband, money, a house, a housekeeper, clothes, furniture, a car, a place at the point-to-point, a night at the opera, a visit to the Royal Academy? Hold your tongue and listen to what he says.

Do you want music without ears, scents without a nose, sights without eyes, a bed without love?

A bed! The rogues and rascals wiggle their bums in the sky.

One night they all said, 'We will make a night of it!', and we dressed up and went along the coast. What shall we do? What is there to do?

'Don't forget, we must save those francs for the journey.'

'Five hundred francs each. We should be able to manage on that.'

In a little café we sat around. In the candlelight the doctors looked mellower. They said:

'Let's each write down what we'd like to do, and draw lots out of a hat.'

A ripple of festivity went round.

We all wrote down what we wanted most to do.

'Go to a nightclub.'

'Drive to the next town.'

'Go to the casino.'

'Dance.'

'Bathe.'

Then, there was a pause. The one who was drawing the papers out of the hat blushed, and handed it on. No one knew where to look. What is it? What is it? Uncle Amos reached across and looked. He turned away. The little bit of love was drained from his cardboard face. He got up and went out. The doctors paid the bill. It was all hushed and strained.

'In extremely bad taste.'

'Quite.'

'Who did it?'

'I don't know. I can't understand it.'

'Shocking form.'

'Quite. Could I have that two hundred and fifty francs now, before we go on?'

The rogues and rascals leaned down out of the sky and said: Only the verb works.

The rude word veered like a scornful rocket across the bay.

All right. I accept. The price of life is pain, since the price of comfort is death and damnation. Histrionics are not necessary. Nothing specific is necessary. Not even one rogue with any particular name. Not one rascal.

Now, on the train, returning, the rogue with bleary eyes has a halo because he says, 'Have a brandy. Here is my address.' A sunburnt family offer me apples from their bundles. I am poor. I am rich. The bare bone is sweet.

Victoria Station is golden and anonymous. Angels cavort in the rafters. Loiterers lean like a Botticelli chorus by the ham-roll counter with their tea.

Up the bus steps for a negligible threepence I go to a queen's position. London in a beatific evening light sighs and receives.

The rogues and rascals have radiant faces in the Queen's Head. They rise and welcome me. They raise their stolen hats and buy me a bitter with borrowed cash. They spend their Authors' Society grants in a single evening and are too drunk to speak. They cadge and cheat. With divine machiavellianism they double-cross. But there is still enough love. It flows back faster than they squander it, and as regular as the managing director's salary. The jackets they nabbed while their host lay sleeping shine like saint's robes.

They are received into heaven.

PART SIX

Kinship is Established

PAVING-STONES PLAY THE PART OF THE WATER SNAKES IN THE ANCIENT MARINER

Something happened today.

The wet paving-stones had a diurnal look.

They presented themselves pathetically, pleading that they last so much longer than life. They greeted me as if we were all dust together at last.

Kinship was established.

This happened coming up Sloane Street, while the traffic lights flashed, and black buildings strained upwards, waiting to be noticed.

It was a short Sunday love-affair, with very little pain.

Afterwards, the dresses in the shop windows

leaned towards me like lusty millionaires with generous impulses.

What a reward for giving love to a stone!

It was impossible to be poor that whole February day.

What do people do at 5.30 in the afternoon, when there's an early amethyst sky, and happiness explodes irresponsible and irrepressible into the luminous evening over the weary city?

What if perfection strikes loud and shocking in the Tottenham Court Road?

What if even a squashed matchbox can sidle into your sympathies?

Will a cup of coffee in Lyons do? Will a bitter in a deserted pub?

How can you meet the minute except by continuing to walk down the Tottenham Court Road stuffed with love?

If it is states you go towards, what do you do when you get there? Feel your brittle bones crushed under the weight. Feel the crudity of the body, crusty soul-casing, far too gauche an instrument to express such gratitude.

So, accept the flattery, the benign drink, the heady money-spending.

Now is not the time to sit alone in a room, eating plums, reading Kierkegaard, hammering at your sores.

I skirted the park at Marble Arch, where a few stall-holders and idlers still flirted with the night. I looked in the coffee-bar through the venetian blinds, and saw people merry with the ends of their sociable evenings. Others waited joylessly in a queue for buses.

It was early enough for all these happinesses and miseries to be criss-crossing each other all over London. Those to whom the day is a weight to be borne and dropped for relief at night. Those who come nosing into the evening like dogs kept back too long.

I'm easily in the arms of them all when the bus lurches, when the Underground's too full. I tolerate the toothpaste on their breath. My head lies against their dandruffed shoulders. For a minute, sometimes an hour, I know how to love.

I daren't look into their eyes for fear that they might misunderstand this amazing love, and mistake it for what they so desperately lack. Or question maybe the comforting deceptions they have got used to.

'I think that's very arrogant, Elizabeth. How do you know that man in the Underground isn't far better off than you?'

'I bought that bit of knowledge with my very own pain.'

For a minute, for an hour, my love can cover everything, everyone: paving-stones, John crying on his stool and not examining his errors, David buying me an Underground ticket as if he were presenting me with Cyprus, dead streets where nothing could ever happen, and dark empty streets full of incipient excitement; I could even take loving care of an obstreperous ego, be tireless, always at hand, infinitely precautious.

That man, when questioned, didn't know why he got up in the morning.

'Animal spirits? So that people shall think well of me?'

Oh but to exult at the zebra crossing! To feel your heart break for the fat lady's extra inches! Would it follow after alcoholic excesses, vindictive lovers, envy making oblique thrusts?

I tell you (but you needn't listen), old mother nature's dandelions and man's dauntless ego can not manage things like that in the wilderness of the world.

Don't you suspect? Haven't all those crossword puzzles given you a clue to the law threaded thicker than telephone wires through everything you do, everywhere?

Look at that lady. How trustingly she leaves a cocktail party and goes underground, sitting so unconcerned in the unkind lights and the roar of machinery! What faith in some engineer and some County Council, meeting to bicker and never above corruption!

Yet the trains run, there are public conveniences, and three working telephones at the corner of my street alone; and postboxes just where you might want them to put an urgent message in the middle of the night.

People see all these things and that might reassure them if they doubted their safety stepping into the Tube. But the point is they don't. That lady just sits. Her absolute faith goes unquestioningly by way of the Underground home to her destination.

William James, will you step up here for a moment and give this lady an analogy suited to her?

Gilbert Ryle, speak to these people plainer. What's the use of quarrelsome words without a big thrust? Put the minuscule argument in a footnote and get to the nub.

I'm off to the pub.

John's still weeping on his stool.

'You've got a bum philosophy! But am I glad to see you!'

'Don't cry. Drink up your drink. Have a cigarette.'

'To have seen what I've seen! Know what I know! These eyes aren't ordinary eyes, duckie. No, they've run the gamut!'

* * *

Gathering, gathering the bedclothes round their poor dying bones. Sweet decay. Sweet sweet spring.

It is the roll of matter heaving into heaven in this long painful individual way.

SOMETIMES PITY SEEPS IN EVEN FOR THE SELF-PITYING

There she is there she is up there, shivering on a bough, crouching into attitudes unable to attract relief. Cowering before the blow of life, how can she open to accept the remedy? How can the engine of regeneration ever work?

Pity, take pity big enough to embrace the knobby bough as well as wounds and fears. Stop in the middle of your jig to appease her with your grief. Be ready to forgive, even if her mistletoe miseries are bright-eyed with underground activities.

That she should *need* to beg from the day! To insist on pity when there's the roar of love!

Displaying disablement in the streets was never

a comfortable way of life, even with its pride of craft. And the pennies it gets are paying for more than the day's work.

That she should *need*! This is what breaks so poisonously into the heart.

A PUBLICAN'S WIFE TELLS HER STORY

'When I was five,' Doris said, 'my father left my mother. He was a steward on a gentleman's yacht, see, and one day he just went off and we didn't hear from him again. We didn't worry at first, of course. But then months went by and then years. I was very upset. I couldn't understand. I adored him. He always made a fuss of me. There were five of us and my mother had to go out to work. It wasn't easy, mind you, she used to cry at night. We shared a room with her, my sister and I. I slept in a single bed and my sister who was only a baby, born after my father left, slept with my mother in the big bed. Well, mother struggled along somehow and then one day when I was eleven and it was just near Christmas we went over to my grandmother's – my father's mother that is. Well, I'd always wanted a doll's pram, and even though I was eleven I still wanted one, because I hadn't ever had one because well naturally my mother couldn't afford things like that, and when we got over to my granny's house my brothers just walked in but I rang the bell, because I liked to see her coming, and she opened the door and said "I've got a surprise for you!" and I thought OOH! the doll's pram! and we went along the narrow hall and I kept peeping into the rooms we passed to go down to the kitchen – Excuse me, dear, there's a customer.'

Doris turned her attention to her customer: a boy with his manly seven-year-old face puckered up and staring seriously at a shelf.

'Packet a gum, please,' he said, staccato.

'Well, now, where was I?' said Doris. 'Oh yes, I was in the hall, thinking any moment now I'll get my doll's pram, maybe, terribly excited. Then my granny led me and my little sister back into the front room and there was my father. And my mother was sitting in a chair crying. I wanted to rush to my father and be made a fuss of but didn't like to seeing as how my mother was crying, so I just stood there. But my little sister didn't. She was too young to understand, and my father made a big fuss of her.'

Such a child a man might find, returning to a village, and think: Perhaps she's mine. (Yes, I have a child, brought up in the slums of Leeds.) Men find this loophole out of salvation. Women are cornered into it. They can't desert with all their children on one ocean raft. Forced to look into those unsuspecting eyes emerging so cockily out of chaos, energetic with an idea they've forgotten except for its urgency, what can women do?

Such pressure away from their ease (even if it leads to salvation) runs into their systems an immense amount of poison, just waiting for the attack. If they look for escape they are troubled by a knowledge of what might be involved.

So they struggle on, saying: If I fall, all falls. This

intolerable weight I carry would be divided like a bad inheritance among my young. I wanted, I insisted, that they be blessed with this gift of living. So far so good. Except now, checked, rushed to too much I can't speak plainer. It is dangerous even to speak. I can cry if I must, but I can't die yet. Not yet until the debts are paid. (DV in January, including tax.)

So between worry and action the faces of women fall away. Can they walk off, leaving behind everything spurious, futile, ignominious, love-lack, over those fields mysterious with mushrooms, over the hill spotted with cows shapeless as slugs in the dusk, and reach at last, that evening, ease in a London pub, where faces glow through smoke and sometimes through distracted anguish? Even a slight parole?

No. They must stay. They must pray. They must bang their heads. Be beautiful. Wait. Love. Try to stop loving. Hate. Try to stop hating. Love again. Go on loving. Bustle about. Rush to and fro.

The truth clings on to them and bites into their beauty.

The womb's an unwieldy baggage. Who can stagger uphill with such a noisy weight?

PART SEVEN

Lament of a Maker

But where, woman wailing above your station, is it you want to go to, get to, accomplish, communicate? Can't you be amply satisfied with such pain, such babies, such balancing?

No. No. There's a blood-flecked urge to go even a step further.

Above the laughter, above the miseries, above the clatter of glasses and the cries of children, I hear a voice saying: Isn't there some statement you'd like to make? Anything noted while alive? Anything felt, seen, heard, done? You are here. You're having your turn. Isn't there something you know and nobody else does? What if nobody listens? Is it all to be wasted? All blasted? What about that pricey pain? What about those people. They sit outside this story, but give it its shape. If it has a shape. What about all the words that were said and all the words that were never said?

If it is all to be buried, all just lived through, life becomes a warmish sort of bath, or worse.

Corroded, the treasure lies below, green and obscene and disintegrating and no use for growing plants.

And another anguished thought: the reporters and recorders with their erroneous conclusions will take over. Such people will put down all that lovely exuberance that existed for a while, and which they saw from a hopelessly excluded position.

Because, you see, everybody else is dead. Or almost. The times are vanished. Imperceptibly everything has turned into something else. The living have memories worse than your own. It's all gone. The longing of the excluded was the strongest thing in all that rich going-on.

So the price of careless rapture is a twisted history chronicled by envy.

You were too busy being. And you are too busy now. You couldn't spare the time to note down a few facts: how the sun and silence poured into the big room with the yellow curtains; how everything was never-ending and expendable.

My father must have died as surprised as when he missed a shot at tennis.

He was a cheerful orphan. At least, his mother died when he was six months old, and his father deserted him and went off to live a long way away with a new wife. His old aunt brought him up. They lived in dingy boarding-houses. He finished school at fifteen and went to work in Woolworths. It was in the basement, overseeing packaging. He was very proud to have fifteen girls under him. But sometimes he was caught reading a book behind the packing-cases. When he was old enough, he went to university. But he always said ruefully: 'Do you think I should have stayed there? Perhaps I'd own Woolworths now and you'd all be millionaires.' It was a wildly greedy thought for a moment, for us. But we always said, No, no, proud of a different richness, all those books, and consciousness of an easy knowledge, rarer and righter. It was a huge luckiness, but we never supposed for a minute that it wasn't ours inevitably. When young he went to concerts until he stopped being bored by music, and then he went still until music belonged to him and could be transmitted to us. He went to the YMCA and won cups for fencing. He said: 'I've always been on the side of the angels.' He had no qualms about them, either. Certainly they were on his side. Living in a tent near Toronto and bicycling ten miles to lectures seemed an amusing way of outwitting adversaries like poverty and loneliness, so puny that he felt sorry for them. He knew there was never a hope they could win. He even grappled with love. But children were, he said, hostages to fortune, and they alone began to tax his strength. He still thought he was winning, merely having an extra invigorating tussle, when death caught him.

Death must have been furious not to have been taken more seriously.

And now, now, it isn't only that he's rotting away in the obscene and alien green of Beechwood Cemetery. It's that he's fading and being forgotten in everybody's minds. Mine, mine too. I forget. I forget too. I won't have it. My brother says there are a dozen or more men like him in Canada this very minute. Is this possible? I don't believe it. How could there be? All over and round the world there never was and never could be.

When I heard the news of his death in wartime England, I went on a picnic as I had planned to do before I heard the news. I told nobody. I breathed in the secret smell in that bluebell wood. The bluebells seemed to come straight up with the knowledge of his grave, so close, so deathly fleshy, they were the painful metamorphosis. Your father is now a whole wood of bluebells. Forever and forever that is all you have left.

But anyhow, and nevertheless, what is the use of several thousand years or more? Merely to move in a greater area of time? Everything you were last year is also equally dead. Everything you are this minute flows away faster than a breeze. It takes pain to burn through time, to turn a spot on the wall into the centre of the world, now and hereafter.

God may be at the back of all this. But his ways are inscrutable.

In the meantime, get a furious weapon. A rage of will. Rise above your turmoil. Exert yourself a swirl above the most you can exert yourself. More? Yes, more every minute. Ounce by ounce. Inch by inch. This is the cruel Lord's will. And the way, too. To be good. Or to make.

Maker, expect no rest. Listen tonight. Above the autumnal winds there's that possibility so wild with hope, battering at the shrugging shoulder and the pooh-hooing diffidence. Brave a night like this and win a prize, you simply can't imagine how big or how reverberating.

All times are these times, and you get to a bony pole of truth in the end.

A pen is a furious weapon. But it needs a rage of will. Everything physical dies but you can send a mad look to the end of time. You can manipulate the bright distracting forever-escaping moment.

But not if you revolve back to a slushy need for love on every side: to be smothered and suspended and surrounded in over around and by it!

But it's a working condition, that's all; a simple scrubbed table to begin a meal upon.

Well, keep your eye on the object, then. And keep your hand moving. Whatever you say will be far far less than the truth. Don't let this dismay you. This is life on earth, where everything is crumbling back into shapelessness, and shapelessness is the great life-giving bog.

You understand, today it is only chaos I am wrestling with. Later this evening it will be a fairer battle. That is, of course, if the evening is kind. If that powerful and beneficial blackness will have me on its mind.

Well anyhow night falls. I'm grateful for these regular choruses. Even the return of pain is comfortably patterned.

'I'm going for a pint.'

'I could do with a pint myself.'

'See you.'

'See you.'

Saturday night and the clerks breathe freely. By an amber whisky mist their faded eyes are shielded from the sight of their submission. Intimations of wild other lives sway their limbs in barbarous rhythms.

O to leap into chaos.

The fathers throw all overboard, and indeed they're wise to do so. Whose will survives the seven days set in spirals of whirling time? Not the worried burdened. It's enough if their strength holds out.

Have you done the dishes? Is the fire still in?

And all the while those kingcups were in that watery part of the wood.

It's several months since you last looked out of the window. There have been two litters of pigs, and the village children are giggling into girls. The green of the trees is getting brown now, like a maturing woman's skin.

It's just service now, and serviceability. But don't look back. If you haven't used the spurt of spring, you'll have to wait till the year comes round. Go about your business. The spur of necessity will keep you trotting about.

Yes, but their dying faces, dying in my dying memory too . . .

'Mother, mother, my soul's on fire.'

'Yes, dear. Is that a new little pimple I see appearing? Shall we try milk of magnesia?'

'The woods were burning with autumn. The blue-jays were wild with foreboding. I was frightened of the future.'

'Don't moon about by yourself in the woods. People will think you are queer. Learn to arrange flowers and take some interest in the house. Be a perfect little lady always.'

Exiles are dreaming over their evaporated milk and tea. Nettles are round the door.

Child lying stiff on one elbow like a frozen prayer, don't listen to chaos below. Will vigilance avert calamity? Relax into innocence. Go and cry in a secret part of the wood, where a wild clematis will compensate for pain. Build a bush house and kiss unresisting worms. It rains and you are enveloped. The wind blows and you know what you face. The mud reminds you of the comfortable beginning of the world, before the immense edict shrugged us into isolation.

For however birth washed you clean, you have only to look up into your grandmother's misted eyes to receive your guilt:

'I won't be here to trouble you much longer.'

'You'll be sorry when I'm dead and gone.'

A gold watch and a pair of buttonhole scissors remain.

Usurper!

But soon usurped.

* * *

'But surely, Betty, it can't have been as bad as that. Why, you girls had a wonderful childhood. Your parents kept open house. No one could have been kinder. You girls don't know how lucky you are. Your grandmother too. Why, Miss Kady used to come every Tuesday and put her hair in tight little snow-white curls. She looked as pretty as a picture.'

On the screened-in veranda, where tea was served on a trolley, in a silver teapot, with cucumber sandwiches, cheese cakes, angel cakes, cookies, and cinnamon toast, sometimes the mournful tones of Bob Devlin's saxophone wafted through the talk, and the ladies were as disturbed as if he had lurched into their midst. ('He drinks, my dear, he drinks.') To a child such desperation coming across the lake explained itself. There perished an early pioneer, born in the wrong place, in the wrong time, without a furious weapon.

Well *get* a furious weapon.

Look how the springs are whirling round and you with your hat askew, without time to catch your breath and decide that THIS is the hour. Lying like an immobile amoeba, gigantic, out of season, and idiotically waiting for instigation. You know this can't be. Leave the washing up and take a look around.

PART EIGHT

Caught up with the people and the dangers they have passed

A BAD NIGHT IN SOHO

I sit at a table at home. I know nothing. I have nothing to say. But the need to say it nags on.

Other people must know more, I think. Who? Who is whirling on in virtuosity and can throw a brilliant sudden torch into this obscure bog where I don't even jog on? Or who lies mud-prone too but has strength enough to raise a bloodshot eye and say, 'Ah yes well that's the way it is.'

I raise my eyes to the books and say, Well, *they* were here and whirl around still all over the western world, which means that their followers-on must too, for nothing stops so suddenly. Are they hidden in veils or strait-jacketed by domestic lives or hammering at their sores in lonely rooms?

The telephone rings.

A reprieve! I think. A friend!

I rush out into the night.

In the pub an elderly maladjusted sailor waves his giant ego about. David nervously fans the flames with polite romantic ministrations. The juke box jollies all along. There is noise. There are other people, anonymous. The landlord is inscrutable, but not god-like. His son is tritely genial. The wallpaper is new and a misunderstood imitation *House & Garden*. The ceiling has push-bell buttons all over it, which boggles the mind if you look up. Sunday boredom is everywhere under the bright neon lights.

I accept a drink. I hope there is someone here who knows something.

I try to enter into the spirit. To give, sympathize, entertain. I think: their needs may be greater than mine.

I suffer. But I haven't the courage to direct things my way or withdraw tactfully when I see how they are going to be.

We tend the sailor's ego.

Pastime for an idle Sunday evening? Social work?

David's position is far from mine. He is getting me and the old lag off his conscience: a social debt is being paid. The old lag is content. Well, naturally.

I get depressed.

This all costs me ten shillings, and them plenty, too. Seems a terrible waste.

I could *do* something. They might be grateful if I insisted on something: demanded, flirted, dramatized, recounted. Yes indeed! Anything makes a change!

But boredom paralyses my faculties. And the possibility of charity stays my hand. Am I needed to say Hurrah to an old friend? God knows I often need that myself, and need it badly. Such friendly tit-for-tat make the Soho nights roll round. But this doesn't seem to be the case here. My urgent interest would be incomprehensible to them. Pride rises up and says Better be bored than bore.

But look how ruthless other people are, following faithfully the rigid roads of their own neuroses. Why can't I insist on what suits mine, instead of standing there and standing there with this hopeless boring neurotic egotistical middle-aged sailor, having my strength slowly syphoned off, for nothing, for nothing at all?

There's the rub: the untenable position of love. Of love.

'To live in a barn beside your mythological castle' (see K)! Well at least I haven't done that.

Is it a mistake to try to BE: good, kind, considerate, a bolsterer-upper, etc., etc.? Perhaps it is impossible to be as well as to do. Being and doing: parallel lines that can never meet.

In this dilemma I hesitate. I accept another drink.

David's well-known well-loved neurosis has taken a strange shape suddenly. Now, with passion, persistence, relentlessness, even, he is worrying on about Mr Butlin's advertising. Well, really! I'd worry about it for a huge fee; but for David, Mr Butlin's advertising problems seem curiously to touch some clitoritically vulnerable spot in him.

Does love order me to worry with him, forget personal urgencies and give him this bizarre necessary something which is sympathetic worry about Mr Butlin's problems, while my despair lies crying below?

It does. I do.

Another night lies squandered.

Not all nights in Soho were great.

Afterwards, what a relief! There is luxurious sinking back into sleep, lovely deep undemanding undisciplined sleep. (Plus dreams, of course, but never mind.)

Upstairs, those sweet undemanding children are asleep too, and they are, I think, I suppose, I hope, cheering me on . . . if . . . and when . . . but how?

There aren't any nose-to-the-grindstone scientists on this job, are there? Who's to know anything? Who's to care two hoots?

Some stories tear aside the veils that cover other people's pain. I heard a woman say:

'My mother died of drink. When I was thirteen she used to send me to fetch a bottle of whisky every day. She had one hidden in each room in the house. "Mother's ill," they said. But one day in the lavatory it came to me in a flash: "She's *not* ill, she's DRUNK!" I hated her! She got more and more hopeless, going round the house supporting herself by the furniture, or incompetently pushing a half-hearted broom. She had a fourth child, an idiot. I used to have to bath it. It was what they call a Mongol. The doctor said it would die and he was right. It only lived seven years.'

Supposing you imagined, going down into the gulf of the Underground, that you were being borne along the birth gulley, out into the new world, amazed, for the first time. Then, then tremendous things might happen. People's faces would astonish. Everything would delight, because it would have no connotations, no history, no meaning but its looks.

Nothing is known. It is merely a comfortable deadening to think anything's familiar; it is an expedient blotting-out of an inherited estate that's far too big for you.

The peasants are watching you, landlord, as you grow over-confident.

Going to the office, riding a bus, standing jammed with your nose to the Tube door, are unique tremendous occurrences, never to be truly known, never even to be partly understood.

'That's a load of Celtic crap!'

'You live in a dream world!'

'Zombie! Zany! Only these eyes have run the gamut!'

'I'd buy you a drink but I have no money.'

'The beauty of it!'

'The boredom!'

'Buy me a drink!'

'I would but I have no money.'

'Broke. Broke. Everyone's broke tonight.'

'To have seen what I've seen! Know what I know!'

The evening rises and rises. Crescendo! Con brio! Anguishes and anxieties whirl away up into a loud Dionysiac chorus, and the moment hangs like a golden bursting ball.

Yes. Those were the days when we razed sacred temples with Dionysius egging us on. We spoke out of tempests! We penetrated the mysteries! We strode the world like colossi! Can you ever forget our iconoclastic ecstasy?

Quiet. Please be quiet.

The diabolical god has gone. And now a million mini-builders, using their mini-road-drills with puritanical fury and vindictive zeal, are rioting round *my* temples, which I need for enduring this frail pale day.

I'll never drink again!

Neither will I!

I saw you looking in the door of the Caves de France, bouncing boy from Glasgow. But as I looked you had become an old old shrivelled man. All in the twinkling of an eye.

But I could have told you it would be like this.

You should have said to death, 'O Death, it is better to keep you in mind', remembering every moment how short time is, and what a concentration is necessary to get you where you're going, or where you hope to go.

As you grow older you see people come up to you in pubs, out of the past. They bring lessons, but mostly pathos. And you see what you were once afraid of cowering there, now to be protected.

AT GRIPS WITH A BOSS

Mr Grip, my one-time boss, cut a hole in the wall, to check my lunch-time absences, and to pass through urgent papers.

It was legal harassment. But Fowler calmed my nerves, and gave me authority to champion semi-colons, sentences ending in prepositions, puns, jokes-within-jokes, all new to Mr Grip, and to shoot down elegant variations and pompous obscurantism. I shot to kill.

'What do you live for then?'

'I've heard that sort of question before. Something similar among my Chelsea friends.'

'Really? What did you answer? Have you heard Voices too? Such sighing under the eaves and across the meadows (Virginia Woolf's may have come from a worse place), such sighing, I say, cannot be struck into accurate fact: the dates, the data of movement, can certainly not be established. I suppose you think shooting stars are transient? Out of sight out of mind, Mr Grip, I expect you know the saying?'

That paragraph is silent, but Mr Grip eyes his whips.

'But what are we playing and can we afford the stakes?'

Silent again. But on a graph a wrinkle of pain.

Mr Grip smiles, is pleased.

Across the Golden Square goes a gallant one-man band, mournful and merry under the August sky. A great Italian mama sits on a bench, benignly smacking the toddlers back, but they always make straight for the puddles, tireless as their two-toned ancestors climbing out of the sea. The big tree leans imposingly, black with age and urban dirt, remembers Hazlitt, sheltered Canaletto, sends old leaves floating as far as Eros.

It's August, so blanched, so near the nub, when, out of heat and boredom, nations declare war. A dangerous time to be sitting, hot and forgotten, bound to desk and duties, bullied into paralysis, under the second-floor window.

This day that was to last forever drops already its dried leaf.

See what happens to whores. No good words will marry them.

'That's not good, Elizabeth. Go back to your sprightly magazine articles and please us better. Don't get above yourself.'

Shame inflames my hard-tried pride. Avuncular Fowler holds my hand till the waves subside.

The tots are shooed home, crying for wet puddles. *They* never give up. Their urge transcends smacks and slaps. Buttered pasta will soon make them forget. Until the next time. Or until the puddles run dry.

Mr Grip takes down his whips, makes a selection, take one homeward bound.

'Fancy, Mr Grip! Whips are exciting?'

'Bullying is too. Two jobs for the price of one.'

AT GRIPS WITH A VICAR

This hole in my side had never been so deep
But Quia amore langeo

The vicar shifted uneasily. God is embarrassing even to a vicar when he's dressed in embarrassing verse. He's all right decently wrapped.

Once a month the vicar throws him off, and recklessly throws off his own fine fig leaves, grasps the maid, and calls her a dirty slut.

'She's a loose woman. Have no more to do with her. Besides, you are ruining the market, paying her ten shillings a week. She's only an Irish peasant. She goes with married men. She's a bad bad girl.'

Bang! Bang! go the whips and cocks and concatenations of Church and State, shaking the crouching people, jostling their prayers.

But the maid is called Mary, and laughs like Mary Magdalene. She smiles and forgives the vicar his tricks and his dreary needs. She finds her kind, is better loved. She shrugs off syphilis, has her hair permed, and goes gaily towards her end. For her, by her, it was feared but unknown. She felt it coming with her Celtic psyche. Fantastic, but such things happen. She was murdered by a famous murderer. He murdered so many so successfully, that she was not even mentioned, just an also-ran. Ran, but couldn't escape, oh gentle generous loving lovable Mary, warm welcoming maid, a shooting star, transient but not out of mind. Never. Rest and shine in peace.

That boss, that vicar, are left to Managing Director and God, till the hypothetical Day of Judgment or a long sleep overtakes them. They're both fired, anyhow, out of my mind, out of my life, forever.

On on I go, escaping whip and pew, only a bit impaired, for these were only short incarcerations, with very little pain.

AT GRIPS WITH A PSYCHOLOGIST

The industrial psychologist prods with an uninterested finger the surface of my subconscious. Office lights blaze bitchily, as he puts his transcendental questions. The mind splashes out like the Rorschach test.

What a tedious job, his drooping manner says, at the end of the weary day!

Are you snooping for the enemy, sir, or just doing your job, trying to find out who is suitable for an advertising agency?

Who would, could, be suitable?

Who works from nine to five unless he has to?

How many marks would Machiavelli get?

Would the doodle on the telephone pad reveal Botticelli?

Even with brandy and candlelight, rehearsed questions go as dead as rehearsed answers, for non-actors. *All all of a piece throughout. Thy chase had a beast in view.* Second time round the lies bite into the truth.

'What is your greatest ambition?'

'To sleep for a thousand years.'

Night after night the newborn baby cries. Night after night the morning comes too soon.

'You're not the vigorous thrusting person we have in mind. We want more go. We want unfailing recipes for life, art, government, and advertising agencies.'

'Then want must be your master, my dear. Goodbye.'

I'm off to the pub, where X is the unknown, and deuces are always wild.

'Are you suffering?'

'The world's worst hangover!'

'A brute!'

'A really vicious one!'

'I was drunk as a fuggy last night!'

'The hell with it! Let's have a hair of the dog.'

PART NINE

The Story of our Life

Once upon a time there was a woman who was just like all women. And she married a man who was just like all men. And they had some children who were just like all children. And it rained all day.

The woman had to skewer the hole in the kitchen sink, when it was blocked up.

The man went to the pub every Friday, Saturday, and Sunday. The other nights he mended his broken bicycle, did the pool coupons, and longed for money and power.

The woman read love stories and longed for things to be different.

The children fought and yelled and played and had scabs on their knees.

In the end they all died.

* * *

Do you insist on vulgar details? Mere gossip? Loathsome gluttony! Very well.

Chapter one: they were born.

Chapter two: they were bewildered.

Chapter three: they loved.

Chapter four: they suffered.

Chapter five: they were pacified.

Chapter six: they died.

I knew a woman who loved a man who trusted the world too much. He bought a fishnet far too coarse, and porridge and morphia became the centre of their lives. She slept with sailors and cried when she scrubbed the floor.

But that's not the point.

In my first labour pain I thought amazed: 'This happened to Nini Keefer too, who used to be scared of the dark and screamed when she stubbed her toe!'

Whatever their names, all those early girls will be patting their double chins, now, panting on the stairs, easier to please.

You're too old now, my dear.
And I'm too old too, my dear.
Our faces are full of flaws.
The truth bites into our beauty.

In the smeared glass jar are two ecstatic newts in a long immobile embrace. Sometimes with slow understanding they make an imperceptible movement towards each other, perfectly balanced on their twig; their eyes outward, their snouts upward, their tails curled permanently like teacup handles.

Is it their pale glowing colour that brings primaeval memories, or their frozen rapturous dance, poised above the decaying vegetable matter, the mud and stones, and the wet snake in the bottom of the jar? So private a preoccupation, so regardless, stirs up dreams of perfection, so sad from where I stand.

Owls are about. A cat complains. Children murmur with bad dreams. The walnut tree sways in a burdened way. The cart tracks wander suggestively off into the horizon. The pigs bang their pens.

Now it's dark. Just intermittent owls.

'Poor woman, that cough's killing her.'

'Left with all them kiddies.'

'Keeps them clean, though, I will say that for her.'

'No word from her husband?'

'Not these five years.'

'Can't they make him pay?'

'No one knows where he is.'

'Mum! Mum! Why is that lady's nose so red?'

'Ssh! She's got a cold.'

PART TEN

Fear of Failing

A STRANGE DREAM

A strange dream happens, and keeps happening when times are worse.

There was a small domestic castle, brushed over pale orange plaster inside, with small unsteady spiral staircases of stone leading down to cellars that were happy, but full of lonely anguish.

Outside in the beech woods, when the leaves were small and calligraphic, loped a troupe of half-grown boys like deer, with bodies the colour of sunlight on bracken, and black eyes, and thick straight hair. They were light-footed, swift, and evasive, but when a soft moon hung on the edge of the horizon, they came stampeding towards the stone castle as if they were all hooved.

I stood upstairs at a window and prayed that this

galloping herd would not crash into the walls. They veered to one side, and their sound grew fainter until the woods appeared safe.

Safe, but apprehensive. That evil orange swelling moon hung expectantly. The overgrown maple bushes on either side of the muddy track stirred ineffectually.

A cart, such as farmers use, clattered up with destructive wheels, driven heedlessly by melodramatic characters. Then turned, and rushed away.

In spite of the bent and broken bushes, the devastated privacy, a moment of relief was apparent. The air had just time to breathe normally between this reprieve and the inevitable cyclic return of the boys.

They came. With savage grace and royal silence, careering with a cruel panther purpose. Oh their wild terrible untouchable beauty!

I tried to hurry down the worn steps to the cellar to rescue that lost child, sobbing forsakenly, but the cry came from an unidentifiable spot.

A weak quiet light started through the small top windows, sunken in the massive walls: a peaceful promise from the contented past, like a wild rose in a disused lane.

O Mother, this body is your house, inconsolable, anguished, dark, mysterious, and happy. If I can bear this onrush, this excruciating pain and ecstatic fear, it will be a castle I can hold. Would I dare then, in the face of a naked mystery, to sweep those stairs and put up gingham curtains? Knit bootees to avoid awe?

Though the floorboards break in the upper attics I will hold on quaking. I will approach the boys with messages and tame a force whose source is eternal. If there are tears left they flow from a secretion no longer so haphazard. Pity hoping for nothing is not so much brave as propelled by a power of understanding, coming like a wave through the bramble bushes to the wounded puma with love.

But I do not understand the subterranean channels of this dream.

Cornered. That's the problem. All your children on one ocean raft. Whose hands can be cut off?

What can be said without the indelicacy of boil-squeezing?

Is it possible to be a bit braver? Is it possible to skirt round the knowledge of your own ignorance, your half-lit fear of what might be at stake?

It's a natural trick to draw a veil over necessary slaughter. To pray, as you walk towards war, for appeasement. To practise side-stepping secretly.

Otherwise, be oblivious. It's not for you to know. Come come come come and deliver me out of this curious nervous anxious moment into the next one.

John's still weeping on his stool.

Robert's still calling for his hole.

David's still worrying about Mr Butlin's advertising.

Night has fallen, comfortably patterned like pain. Night has fallen and provided a shady covering under which I can partly camouflage my big pitted oozing whiskery face.

What if love trickles out through the enlarged

pores? In that case it will cleanse the contours. But through no virtue of your own, mind you. No, not at all. Merely a buttery-fingered effort of God's. And nothing to do with your deserted screaming forsakenly dreary unproven gifts.

But never mind. Night has fallen. Crouch expectantly, and you never know, God might take pity on you and send you a batch of messages suggesting the foolish little thought you invoke so much too furiously.

Expect mercy, but lie down for the rod.

Pray for rain to wipe out all the stains.

My fitted sheet on the line, filled out by the wind, brings to mind an old ship, and the lift of the heart when the wind took her sails and she was off at last. A sense of purpose! Going somewhere! Into the tempest. Extravagant courage. Hopes so high. Seas so cruel. But they knew their jobs and their muscles were hard and obedient. And they thought: I can do it! I can do it!

('I can do it! I can do it!' said Claudia, aged two, when I tried to help her take down her pants. Pride and a challenging look solicited my amazement at her newfound accomplishment.)

I can do it! I can do it! I think I'm going to be able to do it! I feel the first inklings of a breakthrough. What bliss. The ferns immediately assume a startling beauty, and a sense of richness permeates thickly all round.

But don't force. Constipated or not, respect the rectum. (Analogy.)

But the body, the body, the perishable instrument through which all work and visions have to trickle! Assailed by the cold the heat the hunger the exhaustion the heaviness. The difficulty of coddling it on, making it work, keeping it sweet, keeping it clean, condoning its decay, trying not to regret its earlier phases. It's only the body! ('It's only money!') But not to belittle it. Not to misunderstand it. Give it a chance. Urge it on when necessary. Try to be kind to it.

But what a daring thing to do, God: to make such a flimsy, vulnerable, decayable, corruptible, demanding delicate casing for the soul (spirit).

Washed within by the fierce cruel uncontrollable liable-to-frenzy waters of the emotions (psyche).

And all topped off with the complicated wildly-susceptible-to-disturbance computer of the mind.

Wasn't it a fantastic stroke of genius on the part of the Almighty to take such a foolhardy chance?

Is it proving justified?

I *think* so.

Do the turtles fare better, go farther?

No. It's the possibilities of this flayed squashable breakable instrument – just *because* it's so exposed, so open, so killable, so able notwithstanding to receive a million million divergent messages at one and the same time, while struggling on, while coping with the caring, cleaving, suffering, feeding needs.

Of course, there's great wastage. Centuries of leaves make the loam in the forest.

Let's try to evoke a wild rich gaiety. Let's have some fun. I don't mean bitter fun, gruesome frolics. No:

real fun, when the laugh seems as if it will last forever.

A young girl steps out into the dance with a rapt look.

The Roberts greet with a wild joy the whisky and the grave.

A three-year-old boy leaps with rapture as the aeroplane takes off into the skies.

The endless opportunities for joy that take you unawares, releasing you unbelieving like a bird into uncaged freedom. A bonus! (O my dear Franz! Just one more dance!)

'Did you get your hole?'

(Beckett found only a dingy slit, and the breasts hung down deflated and anyhow one of them was missing.)

Now I'm at the centre of the world again and nothing else matters and everything is all right and a benevolence flows down over every petty pre-occupation and idiotic anxiety and irrelevant interruption and the painful paralysis is as nothing and how can it ever have been?

And soon, if I need them, I can summon throngs

of characters, and the little chains of events, and the immortal moments.

And if they should prove to be unnecessary, then they will be concentrated into a rich epithet, but not forgotten.

A FORGOTTEN CANADIAN CALLS

'Put me in! Put me in!' calls Harry Osborne from his thin shallow grave. 'Tell them H.O. was here!'

I will. I will.

Will you recognize yourself in a dapper little felicitous adjective adorning what may seem to you to be merely my unnecessary egotistical unwholesome feminine moan?

Or you may be reflected in the lightness and elegance of a throwaway joke.

Although at eleven I may have somewhat despised your transparent social ideals, you were an artist at after-dinner speeches. And although you insulted me by giving me a lecture on manners when I was seventeen, I will honour you if I can. You didn't know where I was going or what I had to do, and of course you thought your way was best, having won it with your own hard discipline and pain. I know. I know. I saw it all, even through my resentful gawky adolescent eyes.

It is people like this who rise and ask to be spoken of, and not those (or perhaps him) who made the great cataclysms. Because that is something done and accomplished, the glorious deed, the triumphant bee in the orchid, that is never to be regretted, but done done done. It can be ticked off the life-long list.

Not so these unattached Canadian characters, flickering unfertilized and unaware, by the incongruous void.

No. Or maybe no . . . Perhaps a polite little nonentity . . .

('Nonentity'! Shame! Hey love, come here, look! she's saying 'Nonentity' – that's bad, wicked, and untrue!)

I retract.

This slight polite character, who threw his considerable all into being slight and polite, can perhaps lead me gently to the greater characters waiting to destroy me on the way. My compère into hell. Beautifully groomed, beautifully dressed, with smooth snow-white hair, and small stature, and well-rounded, well-arranged phrases for speeches after dinner.

But all the same those times are gone without trace: my father my mother my sisters my brother the houses and the streets and the sounds and the ways, gone, without trace.

And now, only an unbalanced lady in a flower-trimmed hat and mink cape, and a blue-jeaned universal girl meander in the sun in an unrecognizable Sparks Street.

Somebody's hand has been at work. But I don't see the mind behind it.

The blue hills beyond the river, still shaped the same, but not the same at all when you get up close. The lakes so still, untouched, and sweetly breathing, with the crashed old trees reflected round the edge since centuries, now violated.

Clatter of cocktails from the wooden verandas. Cries of kids in outboard motors driving the ancient cries of loon and whippoorwill away.

But why should I be surprised? I expected that.

But not the enormous motorways in and outside and around the town – an effect of concrete and loneliness and a total out-of-touchness, a bulldozing over the old cosiness, crazy culpable cosiness, but workable, maybe, a little human tittle-tattle and acceptable back-biting and understandable refusal to gaze on ungainly horrors.

Who's helping whom to see or love or bear the inescapable? There's no neutral ground. No drinking ease. All to be done alone.

Who's calculatedly isolating these people lost below the Pre-Cambrian shield, and telling them there's protection in a hat and gloves?

Enough of that superficial look at a Canadian city. Let time pass. A thousand more years of pine needles dropping in the violated forests. A million more rapes of lakes.

Nobody's outside the law.

PART ELEVEN

On, on

TRYING TO WRITE, TRYING TO SURVIVE

The breakthrough is a bit bogged down. But on, on. Nibble away at the dam, the dyke, the block, the boredom. It will pour. The worry will be paper enough. Look after the paper. Nappies too; though you can never really believe that a baby will come out. The dichotomy!

('Where did you get your charity?' Where *did* I get my charity?)

Passing through degradation (also humiliation), walking down the Brompton Road, the realization hit me like a bullet, of my child's plight, lost in the dark dangerous city, the wicked morbid men taking advantage, the defiling of the innocent, the diseased grabbing of an opening unsuspecting flower.

This was the blow that laid the boxer low, never to rise again. This was the erasure of the record. This was the fatal famine at the heart of the walled city that made collapse inevitable. Treachery! Vile treachery of those repulsive Furies!

(Oh that hermit thrush! The heavy windless rain! Thuddy drips. And then that double chimey call, song, deep in the wet woods, hundreds of centuries old!)

I suppose we need a drama. Well, a climax, not to say an orgasm, to make an experience – a rising to a height, and a subsiding.

There will have to be a few humans? Snapped in action? Identifiable? They are usually called for, wanted, found necessary for a story.

But there's only me. Large as life.

Pity flashes a snapshot of them caught in their dangerous surroundings, brave and doomed and idiosyncratic.

The body (see above): whatever I said, I fear we must abuse it just a trifle if we are ever going to make a statement. Because *it* only wants ease and absence from shock, and comfort, and the strength to go on; and shies off efforts that might hurt it or leave it overlooked. Its needs conflict with ours. It is not amused by the muse.

Thence cometh the catatonic?

If not, then *whence* cometh the catatonic?

From too many directions? Go one way and wham jam back to the roundabouts, round and round the repetitions until old age strikes you feeble.

Then, there is having forbearance. For bearing what? A kind, catatonic silence, it could be argued.

O excruciating sound of silence yelling!

Hot sun, flowers: useless. Busy birds flitter about. Butterflies lurch past. Dusk falls and finds the old pro in a cagedness, with a cageyness, an alas an alack, a drowsiness, a sinking into ooze, that in spite of memory's glum face seems to have been among the familiar enemies these fifty years. The body lies old. The ego has flown.

Is ego a prick to the muse then? What prick

could prick this old hermit crab? A discipline? Is discipline an amusement? Does pride hide below that shell? Hide all?

Deliver me. From evil? This is?

I am reminded of Philoctetes agonizing on his lonely isle. Left there because he stank. Immortal because of a running sore. All that self-pity didn't matter, apparently. Is this a bit of Greek wit about the muse being no respecter of persons? Art blesses disgusting Philoctetes and his lucky malady. But remember, he had the Bow.

But what about those clearings in the woods, and the wiped-out pioneers, and the lonely women agonizing at their too-far-off water holes? The long meaningless care of their outdoor lavatories? The pain flits about the black-eyed susans, the unrestrained grass, and the young spruces now at last intruded rudely into the window frames. No names. No. But what's a name? Anybody can feel those past people; their ghosts hit you hard as you come bursting out of the dark secretive woods into this little bright patch of total failure.

So, girls, I recommend a study of manure, and

the great rising and falling and fertilizing principles, which are not sad, however many sentimentalists weep to see fair daffodils haste away.

Plants get anxious if they can't fulfil their function. Left alone they always obey the laws. Is it only mankind who is given permission to disobey? That seems to be the implication behind so many religions: you wanted it; you've got it; now get on with it. But millions are hard of hearing, and missed this message, and keep wringing their empty hands, and biting their useless nails.

Is this planned in its turn to give rise to fellow-feeling, human pity, and thereby to be a help to at least a portion of the rest? 'And then they learned to love one another' . . .

The greed of plants to succeed doesn't seem at all disgusting. They don't need praise or encouragement or stimulation (though they often get it). The message, for them, IS them.

But not for me. Having screamed for distraction I am driven to the scary white page, still (illogically) trembling lest anyone look over my shoulder; when not any, no, no one at all, is here, and it is for that reason that I am driven. Driven to drivel, dribble . . . signs of parturition!

How can Beckett be so witty in his agony? Now I know. Once you start speaking, of course, the agony lessens – memory of it is near, but relief makes laughter. Already tragedy turns to comedy, a better form.

The leaden lumpen possession that is taken of one by a depression arising from a fault, a default, a non-act, a refusal to obey, a denial of the inhibited urge to speak!

Speak, memory.

Memory: is it people, places, feelings, things suffused with merriment, gaiety, excitement, expectation?

The flowers floating luminously in the gloaming can be seen or not seen. They can raise the spirits but not the dead. Do they have to be connected to something threaded to a human? If a painter saw them they might work magic, powerfully, but it would be out of *his* connection. The empty chair makes the widow cry, etc. To the auctioneer it's just a cheap chair.

Speak.

What is it? Glimpses, flashes in the medley, sudden revelations impossible to recall, except for their absoluteness – the rock revealed by lightning. Jog on in the fog. Having seen the vision. Yes, but memory fails. A great protective blubber prevents knowledge from percolating through. Living in the instant, only enough memory trickles through to allow a slight sympathy for others living too. And also, there is this whorey desire to please, to entertain, to coat the nasty lethal pill.

Friend, if I had a friend, would be unimaginable. It's the non-me that leads to the blessed cross-fertilization. Just as it is the unimaginability of God that IS God. Anything I can imagine is me.

Twisting, turning, doubling back. Anything to avoid this costive birth.

It is not a time to speak, you say? What does that matter. When was it ever? Who listens? Who ever listened?

To live, people make up ways to make things possible: sometimes I even understand (with a small sharp compassion) their relationships with dogs. It is not expedient to tell the truth, for you, for them; it is important to have a working arrangement, something that gets you, them, by: to their offices, their surgeries, their rehearsal halls, their notebooks, their night-crying babies, their laboratory experiments, their flagging lettuces.

So, you say, lies make the world go round, pads keep people functioning, the truth is best kept for Sundays, or a mere moment of . . . *in poetas*? . . . *in vino*?

Would I say this? Would I say it is not necessary to fuss them?

I have my own pads, blinkers, expedients.

True, but the point here is that mine work too well.

Speak to me, someone, and not just the sad serial of your unlovedness, your unrequited ego, your naughty lust for power.

For a moment, there, things eased up inside me, as if the boil would could might sometime somehow burst, and the passionate artful truthful poison get out into the timely compost heap in time, in time to contribute its germs.

What's the use of cleverly avoiding rape until you're eighty, and then finding out, after all, the hounds were on a different scent?

The maidenhead lies dusty in the junk shop.

'I'm going for a pint!'

'I could do with a pint myself!'

The evening begins when the Roberts arrive. The villagers smile lovingly. Mrs Skinner buys them a Guinness.

'Evenin' Robert, how's the noggin?'

Mr Proudfoot describes one of his epic victories.

Mrs Proudfoot sits, patiently suffering and decaying.

The old ladies giggle, anticipating kisses and Knees up Mother Brown.

'The beauty of it!' cries Robert. 'The boredom! I want my hole! Buy me a drink!'

Mrs Skinner wipes away a tear.

A lonely ingenuous policeman calls in at the pub, with the flimsy excuse that he's looking for the vicar's lost dog.

'I don't get paid enough,' he says, carefully putting away his half-smoked butt.

Zena stands outside the pub, just where the pub lights meet the darkness, against a frieze of council houses, excited by her first outing since the birth of her fourth child, three weeks ago. She is pale, puffy, flabby, but eager to begin again, soliciting a cosy moment to coincide with some primitive suggestive story in her subconscious. Her mother-in-law, happy, fat, just, detached, sits in a row with her cronies inside, like an aboriginal goddess, letting Zena and all other souls on earth extricate themselves from profound vague ravenous longings. Zena's husband is a sailor and away for months. A council house and women's magazines and even all those babies aren't enough. Still, she's not daunted, and nobody pities her and roughly she does what she should against great odds.

Step over and give her a laugh.

'I had eleven,' says Mrs Skinner. But now she is all alone, and hardly able to afford her pint.

'I never had any,' says Mrs Proudfoot, and one more light flickers out in her ill-lit interior.

Who can afford a pint?

No one, but never mind. Rejoice and adore. It's perfectly, perfectly fair, since what we are paying for is love, and currency comes in many kinds.

You remember the name of an excitement; you remember its measurements; it is reward enough for many a sad forgotten night. It atones for the squashed grass and the empty yards and the shifty escaping fears. Keep the fires in and peel the potatoes in good time and remember to be proud. The children are off to seek their lives with bundles adequately packed.

And there may be more fun to come. Knees up Mother Brown!

But after action, even more action. No peace for the wicked. No peace for the innocent either. Fight off twenty years of mopping up and take a look around.

'I'm illegitimate,' said the woman in the pub one day. 'My mother was a servant girl at a big house. My father was hoity-toity and wouldn't take any responsibility. My mother's sister saw them riding round in a carriage and said, "No good will come of this!" My mother was dismissed from the big house and her parents wouldn't have anything more to do with her. But my grandfather said, "Give me the girl and I'll bring her up." Later my mother married and had five children, but I was never one of the family. Oh well, it makes no difference to me now.' She was a friendly kindly well-mannered woman, able to enrich a passing stranger with her story, her courage, her objectivity. Yes, but even these warm encounters can undermine *my* courage. Why struggle to be a good parent when bad ones can produce successes like her?

But who can afford doubt in the middle of the relay race?

Mind reeling, doubts rankling, I move away and up the stairs to the front of the bus, peering through the bleary windows for signs, enlightenment, direction.

More mysteries meet me wherever I look.

What was that pale couple doing on the office stairs, looking out of the window? They seemed undernourished. They carried a sad suitcase. The lights changed. The buses moved through the mist. The couple parted behind the grit-grey window. But nothing changed in their faces. A weary look. A cold coming on.

PART TWELVE

Pacification

Be. Do. See. (Only the verb works.)

Whip up the ever-wanting-to-be-sagging cells.

Why?

Why not let sleeping pricks lie? If the senator is impotent, so much the better for him. Let him snooze untickled. Get him interested in lullabies. Let him watch flowers grow. Let him enjoy his *sole bonne femme*. Why cruelly whip him into a salacious froth?

O bugger the senator. Why did I drag him in? Oh now I remember. He bought a report of those red nights under Brooklyn Bridge, thus causing a flow of words and money to come. Both thundered near me. I watched, but did not benefit. Memories of Niagara, the falls that sprayed me once when I was young.

Back to the book, where the urge surges. Thrums and drums. Hums and haws. Goes underground. Bangs in the engine ominously. (O for an engineer! Shut up, fool.) Can the engine hold out? Of course it can't. Bang on, fool.

What's it about? What's it all for? No story, no characters, no memory of people, places, things.

Out of all those conversations in the heaving fertile evenings, mind to mind, heart to heart, soul to soul, such clear close views into another's being, with persons known then, and persons unknown then, names, faces, and every single word evaporated to a mere rich residue, a social apotheosis.

As it was in the beginning, it is now, and ever shall be, I suppose. I may have mentioned love of various kinds, but that was just to entertain you. I knew you'd be bored and thirsty without a drink, a tale, a diversion on this bald monotonous route. And if I'd set my mind to it I might have been a lot more diverting. I *should* have been, I confess, and you may well complain. But *could* I? I doubt it. Love is not the point. Love is beside the point. (Side by side? Parallel and can never meet? That's for theologians. But how would they know?)

Those places, people, things, moments were just pretty places to stop. Mitigations. Refreshments.

But the bleak point, the boring truth, the stark illogical necessity is simple as a rose's: the eccentric genes impart their message: Write! and the moving finger writes through gales.

I had to get through!

I had to get through with my load!

I see John lurching determinedly with set jaw up Old Compton Street, blind drunk, like a sailor floundering through sand dunes in the nick of time to the haven of his ship. I wave. But he doesn't see me. He turns the corner as if he were in heavy water; heads due north to sanctuary; those eyes that have run the gamut glued to the moment's necessity.

Thus and so I got my load through.

Thus and so I fall down speechless.

'Speechless, mother? Ha! Ha! Your groans can be heard for miles!'

If I'd made for the hills? If I'd left my burden in the meadow and risked being shot for desertion? Less then of the clever compromise, the mis-used skills, the gifts in the gift of the enemy!

Quiet. Should-have-been, could-have-been . . . there's no certainty there. That's fool's chat. Was there ever a parent who didn't look back bewildered, yoked to unmatching sets of strangers from outer space, each one with urgent alien needs, and say, 'Could I have done better?'

You did, all of us did, each time, each move, the necessary thing, the only thing.

The doubts remain, parental doubts, heavy things to carry about.

Did you consider this when you became pregnant, my dear?

I kept the fires in, and peeled the potatoes in good time, and remembered to be proud. And I tried to be kind to babies, saying: What's twenty years' hard labour for a big begetting sin, a big begetting son?

When it's all over we can talk.

Maybe.

'Miss Smart, you are not the first woman to have had four children.'

I picked these roses because they looked so disgusting, just waiting there for the bees to come and fuck them.

Can love keep free from needs?

Needs are bolting in my garden, lanky and green, irresponsible with unsuitable conditions.

There's a change in the soil. Bold mushrooms will appear for all to see.

I am a girl in trouble. Fie. Make the walls ring with a step coming along my corridor. No, not that. Yes, that. A simple touch. A rocking moment. A movement of peace.

Slap me back to sense.

Idle hands get idle fancies.

Sometimes a shaft of pain comes down out of a tree for no reason at all. Sharp, diagonal, sudden out of a landscape, it finds the vulnerable bit to pierce into.

Happiness is not geometrical, but flows in from all sides wherever you look.

If you are overwhelmed, you might as well relax in the whirlpool. It's winning. All you can learn is ecstatic surrender.

Is it reprehensible alchemy to pleasure yourself with inevitable cataclysm?

Do you call *that* expediency?

To die, but to die with your eye on the need for submission?

No, that's, as they say, God's will.